THE
DRAGONS OF BLUELAND

The
DRAGONS OF BLUELAND

STORY BY
RUTH STILES GANNETT

ILLUSTRATIONS BY
RUTH CHRISMAN GANNETT

RANDOM HOUSE · NEW YORK

THREE TALES OF
MY FATHER'S DRAGON

BOOK 1
My Father's Dragon

BOOK 2
Elmer and the Dragon

BOOK 3
The Dragons of Blueland

Reset edition, 1987
Copyright 1951 by Random House, Inc.
Copyright renewed 1979 by Ruth Stiles Gannett
and Ruth Chrisman Gannett
All rights reserved under International and Pan-American Copyright
Conventions. Published in the United States by Random House, Inc., New York,
and simultaneously in Canada by Random House of Canada Limited, Toronto.

This title has been catalogued by the Library of Congress as follows:
Gannett, Ruth Stiles. The dragons of Blueland. Summary: Elmer must come once
again to the aid of his flying baby dragon when men discover its
retreat and begin to hunt it.
[1. Dragons—Fiction] I. Gannett, Ruth Chrisman, ill. II. Title.
PZ8.G2Dr 1951 [Fic] 51-13557 ISBN: 0-394-91092-3 (lib. bdg.)

Manufactured in the United States of America
1 2 3 4 5 6 7 8 9 0

FOR
SHARLY
AND
PEGGY

WHAT WENT BEFORE

Once a baby dragon flew away from home to ride on a cloud. And he fell off onto a place called Wild Island, hurting one wing so badly that he could not fly back to his cloud. The fierce wild animals of Wild Island tied him to a rope, and when his wing got well, they made him fly them back and forth across a muddy river.

An old alley cat exploring the island saw the miserable dragon. They became good friends, and she promised to help him escape. When she went home she told Elmer Elevator, a brave boy of nine, all about the dragon. He set off to the rescue and tricked the wild animals, cutting the dragon's rope just as the animals were about to catch him, too. He jumped onto the dragon, and off they flew.

Then Elmer remembered that he'd better start back home to Nevergreen City. The dragon offered to fly him, but a terrible storm forced them down over the ocean. Just by luck they landed on a sand bar near an island, and when they waded ashore they found that only canaries lived there. Elmer met an old canary friend who introduced them to the canary king, King Can XI. The King asked if they would dig up an old treasure chest, explaining that he was suffering from the dreadful disease of curiosity and could not get well until he had seen that treasure.

Elmer and the dragon finally found the treasure. Everybody joined in a wonderful celebration, and afterwards Elmer and the dragon flew off to Nevergreen City. The dragon left his good friend on a wharf, and started back to his own home in Blueland.

CONTENTS

Chapter One

THE HIDING PLACE

Over the harbor, past the lighthouse, away from Nevergreen City flew the happy baby dragon. "I'm on my way home to the great high mountains of Blueland!" he shouted to the evening skies. "At last I'm off to find my six sisters and seven brothers, and my dear gigantic mother and father."

He sped northward over the coast of Popsicornia. He flew all night through the dark scudding clouds toward Awful Desert, which surrounded the mountains of Blueland. "I must be careful," he thought to himself, "that nobody sees me on my way, but I'll have to stop and rest somewhere. Where can I hide? I've grown as big as a buffalo, and my blue-and-yellow

11

stripes and gold-colored wings will certainly attract attention."

The darkness faded into morning, and looking down he saw green meadows, fields of corn and potatoes, a road wandering past barns and houses, and a brook zigzagging back and forth across the road. "Perhaps I can find a bridge to hide under," thought the dragon, "but I'll have to hurry. Soon the farmers will be up."

He swooped, and coasted down to a place where the road crossed the brook. Gently he landed and pattered down the bank to hide underneath the bridge. But there wasn't any bridge! The road had been built right over the brook, and the water flowed under the road through a culvert, a long round tunnel. And the culvert was too small for a dragon to hide in.

"I'll try another crossing," he said to himself, scrambling up the bank, and galloping down the road as fast as he could to the next crossing. But here, too, a very small culvert carried the water under the road.

"Oh dear, oh dear!" he muttered as he galloped on farther between a yellow farmhouse and a big yellow barn. Just as he was passing he heard a rooster scream and a window slam shut in the house. "Where shall I hide? Where shall I hide?" he panted.

And then he came to a third crossing. He tumbled down the bank and found another culvert, but a big culvert, big enough for a baby dragon to hide in. He crawled inside, wading through shallow water that cooled his hot, sandy feet.

"What if someone in the farmhouse saw me?" he kept thinking as he stretched just far enough to nibble the tasty skunk cabbages and marsh marigolds growing outside the culvert. And then as he ate and cooled off, he felt tired and happy and almost safe, and he dozed off to sleep in the culvert.

Chapter Two

MR. AND MRS. WAGONWHEEL

But someone *had* seen the dragon. At least he was sure he'd seen something blue and yellow and gold galloping down the road. It was Mr. Wagonwheel, the farmer living in the yellow farmhouse, who had just been closing his window as the dragon ran past.

"What's that galloping noise?" asked Mrs. Wagonwheel, sitting up in bed.

"A large blue monster just ran by, and after breakfast I'm going to find out all about it!" yelled Mr.

Wagonwheel, jumping into his clothes and rushing off to put the cows in the barn for milking.

Mrs. Wagonwheel, meanwhile, made pancakes and coffee, but forgot to boil the eggs. She was horribly upset at the thought of a monster rushing past her house at five o'clock in the morning.

Mr. Wagonwheel hurried through the milking, let the cows into the pasture, and dashed back to the kitchen. He was anxious to eat and be off after the Blue Demon, as he had decided to call whatever it was. He swallowed a pancake whole and banged two eggs on the side of his cup.

Splop! Raw egg flew all over the table and Mr. Wagonwheel. Mrs. Wagonwheel had forgotten to boil the eggs, of course.

"Martha! What's the matter with you?" yelled Mr. Wagonwheel.

"Oh, I'm sorry," said poor Mrs. Wagonwheel. "I'm so upset about that horrible monster I don't know what

I'm doing," and she nervously slipped a pancake instead of her handkerchief into her apron pocket.

"Well, boil more eggs!" roared Mr. Wagonwheel, going to the sink to wash off his face and hands and shirt and overalls.

Now Mr. Wagonwheel liked his eggs hard, very

hard, and as he waited for them to get very hard, it began to rain. It was only a drizzly rain, but enough to wash away the dragon's footprints in the dusty road.

"Drat it!" thundered Mr. Wagonwheel, looking out the window. "It's raining!"

"I thought we needed rain, dear," said Mrs. Wagonwheel.

"We do, but why can't it wait until I capture the Blue Demon? Now maybe I'll never find him."

"Maybe it's just as well," said Mrs. Wagonwheel, carefully putting a spoonful of salt in her coffee.

"Well, I can see you have no spirit of adventure," grumped Mr. Wagonwheel, peeling his at-last-ready very hard eggs.

He picked up his rifle, a strong rope, and put on his raincoat and boots. "I'm off!" he yelled, and slammed the door.

"He'll never come back," thought Mrs. Wagonwheel, and she quietly sat down to cry.

Mr. Wagonwheel ran down the road, pouncing on bushes, peering behind trees, and examining road-side ditches, yelling all the while, "Coming, ready or not!" He made such a racket that the cows heard him in plenty of time. They huddled around the big culvert where the baby dragon was hiding and pre-tended to be busy drinking water. For they had found the sleeping dragon while Mr. Wagonwheel was eating his very hard eggs.

"Wake up!" they had said, "and tell us what you are, and what you're doing in our culvert."

The dragon woke up with a start, and then smiled at the friendly cows. "I'm a baby dragon," he explained, "and I'm on my way home to the great high mountains of Blueland."

"But what are you doing in our culvert?" asked a cow.

"I'm hiding. You see, most people think that there are

no dragons left, and if I should be captured, I'd surely end up in a zoo or a circus, and never get home again."

"Sh!" said another cow. "I think I hear Mr. Wagonwheel now. All through milking time he was muttering about catching a Blue Demon. He must have meant you."

It was then that the cows huddled around the opening to the culvert, and the dragon crouched down on his stomach in the water.

"The culvert!" yelled Mr. Wagonwheel, brandishing his rifle. "An excellent hiding place for the Blue Demon." And he started down the bank on the other side of the road.

"It's all over now," thought the dragon, who could tell where the farmer was from the noise he was making. But just then Mr. Wagonwheel looked across the road at his peaceful cows and thought, "My cows would be in a panic if the Demon were hiding here!" He turned back up the bank and ran down the road, beating the bushes and peering behind trees.

The cows grazed nearby all day long, talking to the dragon and telling him when it was safe to come out of the culvert. Toward evening they heard Mr. Wagonwheel stamping back along the road, yelling "Hoop-la! All of you, into the barn!" and as they wandered off they quietly warned the dragon, "Leave just as soon as he goes to the barn. It's just like him to be out looking for you by flashlight after supper."

And they were right. Long after the dragon had flown far beyond the yellow farmhouse and culvert, Mr. Wagonwheel was shooting into bushes. Mrs. Wagonwheel was in bed with a case of nerves.

Chapter Three

THE MEN ON THE SLOPE

"It's a lovely night for flying," thought the dragon as he hurried toward the north, urged on by cool brisk winds. The rain had stopped long ago, and a crescent moon shone palely. Looking down, he could see the outline of Seaweed Bay, and then a point of land

24

called Due East Lookout. At this point he must turn and fly directly westward over Seaweed City, across Spiky Mountain Range, and over Awful Desert to reach the Blueland Mountains in the heart of the desert. Many people had tried to cross the desert and climb these mountains, but there was no water, and treacherous sandstorms raged all year round, making traveling almost impossible. So far, no man had succeeded.

"It won't be long now!" sang the baby dragon as he passed over Seaweed City, over the coastal Spiky Mountain Range, and then started over Awful Desert beyond.

"What a lovely night!" he thought again. And then, all of a sudden, he realized how clear it was over the desert. "Where are the sandstorms? Yes, where are the sandstorms?" A sick feeling came over him. In weather like this a man might be able to cross the desert into Blueland, might see one of the dragon

family, and learn the dragon secret, *that dragons still
live in Blueland!*

Faster and faster he flew, and way up ahead he saw
a tiny light where the mountains rose straight up out
of the desert.

"Men!" thought the dragon. "If only I'm in time to
warn my family."

Onward he sped until he could see that the light was
the blaze of a campfire on the rocky mountain slope.

He counted four or five men sitting around the campfire.

"I'd better find out what they're planning to do so I'll know how to save my family," thought the dragon, circling down and landing below the men. He carefully picked his way through the huge rocks on the slope and hid close enough to hear what the men were saying.

"If Frank and Albert and the rest don't find water soon, we're sunk. We'll have to get back pretty quick, and what if the weather changes? After all, this is the first time, so far as anybody knows, that the weather has ever been clear over the desert, and I don't trust it to last very long."

"Me neither," said another voice.

Just then they heard a shout farther up the slope and a man came running down toward the fire.

"Did you find water?" they asked him.

"Water! Loads of it. The mountains form a circle,

and all the streams from these mountains flow toward the center to make a tremendous lake. But that's not all we found!"

"You mean you found evidence that the great dragons of Blueland actually did exist at one time?"

"Evidence!" said the man who had run down the slope. "Evidence! Why, we've got fifteen of the most beautiful dragons you ever dreamed of trapped in a cave that seems to have only one entrance. The rest of the men are guarding it."

"Fifteen trapped in the cave!" moaned the baby dragon. "Why, that's my whole family—my six sisters, seven brothers and my dear gigantic mother and father. I'm the only one left to save them. But why didn't they fly away?" He listened to the men again.

"How do you know you have fifteen in a cave?"

"We took them by surprise. They were asleep at the entrance, and when they saw us they rushed inside. What a sight!"

"Fifteen dragons!" One of the men whistled. "What did they look like?"

"They went so fast it was hard to see, but there was one huge blue one, a big yellow one, about five smaller green ones, and the rest were blue and yellow. They all had red horns and feet, and gold-colored wings!"

"I can't wait," said one of the men. "Why, every zoo in the country will want one!"

"Oh, no!" groaned the horrified baby dragon, hiding behind the rocks.

Chapter Four

IN THE CAVE

As the men went about packing up knapsacks and putting out the fire, the dragon carefully crept up the mountain slope. "It's a good thing they don't know that the cave does have another entrance, but I wonder if I can still squeeze through it."

It was the tunnel through which he had gone when he ran away to sit on the cloud. At that time, only he and his two youngest sisters were small enough to fit into it. "Maybe, just maybe, I can still get through," he thought.

He hurried up the dry rocky slope of the mountain, racing to get to the tunnel before the sun broke over the rim of the desert. "I've got to rescue them!" he

thought frantically. Over the gap between two snow-capped peaks he galloped and then down into the beautiful green alpine meadows in the center of the mountain circle. Here, streams babbled down the slopes to a bottomless lake. Masses of wild flowers, gentians, butterfly weed, painted cup, all colors,

paraded along the brooksides. In the pastures, everywhere, were giant snapdragon plants looking more like bushes than flowers, but the dragon did not have time to stop and gaze at his beautiful home in the great high mountains of Blueland. Already the sun was reaching over the horizon, lighting up the sky.

"Here it is," he panted and he dove into a thick clump of snapdragons growing over the entrance to the small tunnel. He had seen the men across the lake guarding the cave with an enormous net. "I wish I knew what they're planning to do next," he thought. "But it's too late now. I'll have to wait until dark."

He tried to pass into the tunnel, but the roots of the snapdragons had grown over the entrance, and dirt had washed in from above. "Dig carefully. They might notice the stir in the bushes," he warned himself as he cleared the way. At last he could fit into the hole, and he started the long trip through the tunnel.

"I might get stuck any moment," he groaned as the tunnel turned corners and gradually dug deeper into the side of the mountain, always only just big enough for him to squeeze through.

On and on he crawled, and just when he thought he would surely get to the large part of the cave, he got stuck. He pushed and wiggled, but he could not get through. Tears rolled down his blue cheeks. "I wanted so badly to see my family," he sniffled. "But maybe they're near enough to hear me now," and he whispered, "Mother, Father, are you there?"

"Who's that?" asked a voice that sounded like his sister Eustacia's.

"It's Boris!" cried his mother. "Oh, Boris, Boris! We thought we'd never see you again. Come on into the cave. We're in terrible danger."

"I know," said Boris the dragon. "But I can't squeeze through the tunnel. Oh, I do wish I could.

But listen, whatever you do, don't go near the main entrance to the cave. Many men are waiting there with an enormous net. I don't know yet what they plan to do with it, but I'll try to find out tonight if nothing happens before then. I think they're afraid to come in and get you. They don't know how harmless we really are. Anyway, keep calm and count on me. I have a

friend who may be able to help, and if you don't hear from me soon, it'll be because I've gone off to get him. Now I'll have to back out again. I must stay near the tunnel entrance so I can get out easily when I have a chance. Goodbye!"

And Boris backed out for what seemed like hours and hours until he came out among the roots of the snapdragon bushes. He peered through the leaves across the lake and counted sixteen men standing in a row outside the cave. A breeze sprang up across the lake and carried their voices over the water to him.

"They'll come out when they get hungry enough," said one man.

"But how do you know they won't be fiercer when they're hungry and have been trapped for some time? Me, I'd rather go in after them right now."

"Go in after them?" said a third man. "Why, we don't even know anything about that cave. Suppose it does have more entrances? The dragons may have escaped already. And what about pitfalls and rockslides in there? We ought to know more about this. No, the thing to do is to leave ten men here on guard, and send the other six to search for other entrances and to have a look at the rock formation around here."

"Good idea!" said the man who had come down the mountain to the campfire.

The wind changed and the dragon could only hear confused sounds of talking, but the men seemed to be deciding who would stay and who would go.

"They'll find me for sure if I stay here, and I don't want to trap myself too," thought the dragon. "Daylight or no, I'd better fly and get Elmer. He'll know what to do, if we can get back in time."

Quickly he fitted the snapdragon roots over the tunnel hole, arranging them carefully so they wouldn't look newly dug-up. Then, keeping close to the ground, he crept through the green meadows and up, up, up to the gap between the mountain peaks. He took one last look at the beautiful blue lake surrounded by the green, green meadows, felt quite sure he hadn't been seen, and then plunged down the rocky slope on the other side. Up in the air he flew, shielded from the eyes of the men by the circle of mountains.

Chapter Five

BACK TO NEVERGREEN CITY

High, high over the desert flew the dragon, the hot wind stifling him, the hot sun parching his throat. He strained his eyes to see each object on the sands to make sure it wasn't a man.

At last he was over Spiky Mountain Range. Panting for air and water, he circled down fast and plunged through the trees to a mountain brook. He had seen no one on the desert.

"I'll rest here until dusk," he thought, sticking his head right under the cool, gurgling water. Then he lay down in the brook on his stomach, carefully keeping his gold-colored wings out of the water. As he dried off on a sunny rock he listened for noises of men and dreamed of how he and Elmer would rescue his family. Once he heard children's voices, but a woman called them together and they went off in the other direction.

"School picnic," he thought as he shook out his wings for the long, hard trip ahead. He wanted to reach Nevergreen City by morning without stopping.

Up through the trees and over Seaweed City flew the dragon. He saw lights popping on suddenly along streets, in houses, but he didn't hear a little boy scream, "Mommy, come look at the dragon in the sky!"

It didn't matter. The little boy's mother only said, "Chester, I told you to stay in bed!" So Chester was the only one to see the dragon, and nobody believed him until later when the "dragon affair" had become famous.

"As I remember, Elmer said he lived right across the street from a park," thought the dragon as he hurried on. "Yes, it was Evergreen Park, but what if I can't find him?"

The wind beat back his tears as he raced over Seaweed Bay, over Mr. Wagonwheel's farm and the zigzagging brook. He thought he could see the road as the moon slipped in and out among the clouds.

He flew to the coast of Popsicornia and followed it southward. Suddenly he felt flooded in light. What had happened? The moon? No. He looked down and saw a beam of light leaping up from a ship off the coast. He violently zigzagged up and down, to one side and then to the other, trying to get rid of the light.

Men were shouting on the ship. Into the beam, out again, flooded in light, out of the beam again he flew. He knew that the ship's searchlight had found him accidentally, but as it tried to follow his flight he thought wildly, "How well can they see me? What do they think I am?"

And then, as suddenly as the light had found him, it lost him. He sped on in the comforting darkness, his heart pounding hard with fright.

As dawn began to break into the sky he saw Nevergreen City harbor, the lighthouse, and in the center of the city, a large green shape.

"Evergreen Park," he thought with relief, and he quietly glided down among the trees. No one had been on the streets to see him.

Chapter Six

ELMER TO THE RESCUE

Dawn brought Saturday to Nevergreen City and as Elmer slept snugly in his comfortable bed he was suddenly awakened by a damp cold kiss on his cheek.

"Wake up, wake up!" insisted a voice.

He opened his eyes and muttered, "It's Saturday. No school today."

"Elmer, wake up!" said the old alley cat, the same old alley cat that had told him all about the dragon and how to rescue him. "Elmer, we've got work to do. I just saw the dragon fly into the park. He must be in trouble. We'll have to hurry to find him a hiding place before the city wakes up."

"The dragon! Why, he only just brought me home!" Elmer jumped out of bed and into his clothes, and tip-toed down the stairs with the cat following behind.

Silently they crept out the front door, down the porch steps and into Evergreen Park. "You look this way. I'll go down the other way," said the cat.

"Where could a dragon hide?" wondered Elmer, looking at the rows of trees along the walks, the scattered rocks, the pool, and then at the place where

the city was going to build an amusement center.
A big steam shovel sat idly on the spot marked out
for foundations. Elmer liked steam shovels and was
just thinking of exploring this one when the shovel
jiggled a bit.

"The dragon!" He climbed up quickly into the cab.

"Elmer!" whispered the baby dragon. "Oh, Elmer!" And the dragon burst into tears because he was so glad to see his friend.

"The alley cat saw you fly into the park," explained Elmer, hugging the dragon around the neck. "But why have you come back? Are you in trouble?"

"Terrible trouble," groaned the dragon, and he explained what had happened to his family. "You'll help me, won't you?" he pleaded.

"Of course," said Elmer. "Let's think out a plan. I suppose we'll have to wait until dark to leave."

"I suppose so," said the dragon sadly.

"But you'll be able to rest right here," said the cat, who had found them by this time. "It's Saturday, and the men won't start today. I'll keep meddlers away. Meanwhile, let's work on the plan."

The three friends discussed the problem all morning. Then Elmer went home for lunch. His mother was used to his long early morning walks, but she'd be suspicious if he didn't turn up for lunch.

That afternoon Elmer took all the money out of his tin bank and went to collect the things he would need. He bought:

16 whistles, of assorted tones
16 horns, of assorted tones
 1 cap pistol, with caps
 1 ball heavy string
 6 large chocolate bars
 3 boxes Fig Newtons

He found his very sharp jackknife, and took a flashlight from the kitchen drawer. Then he carefully packed everything in his father's knapsack and went down to supper. He had $7.36 left over from the shopping.

"Elmer, what have you been doing all day?" asked his mother. "I haven't seen hide nor hair of you except for lunch."

"Oh, I've been over in the park looking at the place where they're going to build the amusement center," said Elmer, which was true in a way.

At last the moment came to sneak out with his knapsack and join the dragon at the steam shovel. As he ran down the path he saw the old alley cat waiting for him. "I'm sorry you can't come, too," said Elmer, climbing onto the dragon's back.

"So am I," said the cat sadly. "But I'm too old. I'm better off taking care of your mother and father. They do worry so. Well, goodbye! Good luck!"

"Goodbye!" whispered Elmer and the dragon as they flew up into the air.

Chapter Seven

THE DRAGONS OF BLUELAND

"Tell me more about your family," said Elmer as the dragon flew over the harbor and northward along the coast of Popsicornia. "Do you all look alike?"

"Oh, no. We've all got gold-colored wings and red feet and horns, but my father is blue and my mother is yellow. All my six sisters are green, ranging from

yellow-green to blue-green. We boys are all both blue
and yellow. I have wide stripes, but two brothers
have narrow stripes, one with the stripes going the
other way; one has yellow polka dots on blue, and
one blue polka dots on yellow; one has a yellow head
and body and one leg, with three blue legs and tail;
one is speckled blue and yellow like a bird's egg; and
the last has patches of blue and yellow."

"How wonderful! You must look like an Easter
parade when you're all out together."

"I guess we do," said the dragon, "especially when

Father has us doing our exercises. He's a great one for exercises."

"Exercises?" said Elmer.

"You know, standing on your head and somersaults and leapfrog and all that sort of thing. Of course, in the summer we spend most of our time mowing the meadows and tending to the flowers. Each one of us has a special part of Blueland to take care of. I wonder what's become of my piece. I suppose Mother has taken it over. I had the marshy part near the lakeside. That's why I'm so particularly fond of marsh mari-

golds and skunk cabbages."

"But what about in the wintertime?" asked Elmer, looking down at the line of waves breaking against the rocky shore in the moonlight. "It must be very cold and snowy, and not much fun for exercising."

"Oh, we do our exercises summer and winter. Father sees to that, and of course we have lots of fun sliding down the mountain slopes onto the frozen lake. But the winter is really fun because we sit in a circle in our cave and Father tells us scary stories about knights. It seems there used to be lots of knights who rode about just looking for dragons. They captured and

killed most all of us, but a few escaped to Blueland. My father says his grandfather could remember the knights very well, with their heavy coats of armor and lances and swords and helmets."

"Oh, sure. I've read about them in books," said Elmer. "But those dragons were always fierce and about to eat up somebody."

"Nonsense," said the dragon. "That's just what the knights liked to make people believe, so everybody would think they were very brave when they went dragon hunting. Dragons look fierce sometimes, but they're really very gentle. That's why they finally ran

away to Blueland. They wanted to be left alone. And now more men have decided to bother us. Goodness knows what they'll do to us this time. If only we get back in time! We can't possibly make it before tomorrow evening. That will make it over two days since I left."

"Oh, we'll save your family all right," said Elmer hopefully. "I can't wait to see them all." He snuggled up against the baby dragon's neck and dreamed of the rescue as they sped through the night toward the mountains of Blueland.

Chapter Eight

TO SPIKY MOUNTAIN RANGE

"Where are we going to rest tomorrow?" asked Elmer, biting off a corner of a chocolate bar to help him stay awake.

"I'm trying to get all the way to Spiky Mountain Range," said the dragon. "No more Mr. Wagonwheel for me if I can help it. He's an awful..."

"A searchlight!" interrupted Elmer as a beam of light shot up from below, lighting up the dragon's gold-colored wings.

"It's from that ship, Elmer. They saw me last night, too. Hold on tight. I'm going to try to dodge it!" yelled the dragon, swooping, diving up and down, swerving from side to side.

Elmer grabbed the dragon's neck and held on as hard as he could. He didn't dare open his eyes, but he could hear men shouting on the ship.

"Right, move it to the right! Faster, faster!"

"Left, now! Hey! I think something's riding whatever it is!"

"Looks like a boy!" shouted another man.

And then the moon slipped behind a cloudbank. The dragon escaped the beam of light, and flew frantically through the darkness while the light danced over the sky still looking for them.

"Good work!" said Elmer, feeling very dizzy and quite sick.

"But they saw us, both of us," moaned the dragon.

"That's all right. They don't know where we're going, and we'll have your whole family rescued by the time they decide what we are," said Elmer, wondering if it would be wiser to finish eating his chocolate bar then or later. He was still feeling sickish.

"I hope you're right," muttered the dragon doubtfully.

On and on they flew until at dawn they were over Seaweed Bay and Due East Lookout. The dragon swung westward over Seaweed City and landed in a forest on Spiky Mountain Range. He was so tired that he fell asleep before he had time for a drink of water. Elmer finished his chocolate bar, ate another, and a whole box of Fig Newtons. Then he drank from the mountain stream and curled up beside the sleeping dragon.

Luckily, they didn't know who had seen them over Seaweed City. Ever since Mr. Wagonwheel had glimpsed the dragon Thursday he had been trying to persuade his neighbors that he really had seen a Blue Demon. No one believed a word of his story, but he had bothered the whole town so much that they told him to report it to the Seaweed City police. He had planned to go on Sunday, but changed his mind in the middle of Saturday night. He woke Mrs. Wagonwheel. "You take care of the morning milking, and I'll be back in time for dinner. I'm taking the horse and wagon."

"But..." said Mrs. Wagonwheel.

"I'm off!" said Mr. Wagonwheel, and Mrs. Wagonwheel heard the kitchen door slam behind him.

So, at dawn, just as he was trotting through the outskirts of Seaweed City, Mr. Wagonwheel looked up into the sky to see what sort of a day it was going to be. And he nearly fell out of his seat.

"The Blue Demon!" he screamed. "With a boy or something riding on its back!" He looked around wildly for someone to show it to, but nobody was in sight. And by the time he reached the police station and had found someone to listen to him, Elmer and the dragon were safely hidden in the forests of Spiky Mountain Range.

Chapter Nine

BLUELAND

Elmer and the dragon dozed on until late afternoon. They were both impatient to be off, but as Elmer said, "We'd only spoil everything by getting there before it's dark enough."

So they waited and rested and drank cool mountain water. The dragon munched ferns while Elmer ate his third chocolate bar.

"I can't stand it any longer," said the dragon,

jumping up and shaking out his wings.

"All right," said Elmer. "Let's go!" He put on his knapsack and climbed onto the dragon's back. They walked to a clearing in the woods, and the dragon took off across Awful Desert.

It was hot over the sands even in the late afternoon, and Elmer crouched over to hide from the burning winds. The dragon panted for air, but flew faster and faster, hardly daring to think what might have happened since he left. He kept muttering, "If only the sandstorms would start up! Where are the sandstorms? That would make the men leave us alone."

When they came to the dry rocky slopes of Blueland the sun was low on the horizon, and they knew it would soon be dark inside the circle of mountains.

"Keep a sharp lookout," warned the dragon as they picked their way through the boulders. "They may have men most anywhere."

Up, up they went, slowly, quietly. At last they

reached the gap between the peaks and Elmer gasped at the sight below him. The beautiful meadows of Blueland shone bright green, dotted with patches of snapdragons glowing white in the dimming light. And at the center the lake water reflected the pink of the sky. Suddenly it was gone into darkness as the sun set.

But the dragon had been straining to see across the lake and suddenly he grabbed Elmer for joy. "The men, I saw the men, and they were still standing outside the cave with the net. Maybe we're not too late!"

He hurried Elmer down to the giant snapdragon bush which hid the entrance to the little tunnel. "I don't think they found it," he whispered happily as he pulled aside the roots and rocks.

"Neither do I," agreed Elmer, looking all around to be sure he'd remember the spot. Then he took off his knapsack and unpacked one whistle, one horn, the flashlight and the ball of string.

"Lower your neck so I can measure the strings for

your whistle and horn," he said, getting out his jack-knife.

"Why do I have to have them on strings?" asked the dragon.

"I don't want you to drop them. If the men never see them, maybe they'll never guess what happened."

The dragon laughed, and tried out the strings to make sure he could reach the horn and whistle easily. "They're fine," he said. "Now I'll wait here until you tell me it's time. Look, the men are building a campfire. They must be having supper."

"So much the better," said Elmer as he started down into the tunnel with his knapsack. "But how will your family know I'm your friend?"

"Tell them Boris sent you."

"Boris! Is that your name?"

"Yes," said Boris uncomfortably. "I was embarrassed to tell you before."

"It's no worse than Elmer," said Elmer.

"I suppose not, and it's certainly not so bad as some in my family. I might as well tell you the rest. My sisters are Ingeborg, Eustacia, Gertrude, Bertha, Mildred and Hildegarde. And my brothers are Emil, Horatio, Conrad, Jerome, Wilhelm, Dagobert and Egmont. Can you imagine! But hurry! I can't wait to hear what's been happening to them all."

Once inside the tunnel Elmer snapped on his flashlight and shot it over the damp walls. The ceiling was high enough so he could walk easily. Down, down he went, around curves, through small rooms and then more narrow tunnels until at last he came to the place

where the dragon had got stuck. He heard scratch-
ing and scraping noises and he knew he must be very
close to the dragon family.

"It's Elmer Elevator, Boris's friend," he whispered
as bravely as he could.

"Who?"

"Elmer Elevator, Boris's friend. Boris is out at the entrance to the tunnel, and I've come to rescue you."

"Turn off your light and come in," whispered another voice, and Elmer walked slowly into the darkness. He stopped, and felt himself surrounded by huge forms breathing excitedly.

"We can't tell you how grateful we are," said the gigantic dragon mother.

"Never mind that," whispered the father. "What's your plan and how can we help? We're almost starved to death."

"Oh, have some chocolate bars," said Elmer, generously giving away his last three. "Here, I'll open them up for you, and divide each one into five pieces. I'm afraid it's not much, but it ought to help a little." He held his flashlight inside the knapsack and divided up the chocolate as he explained his plan. They all chuckled low dragon chuckles and began to feel much better.

Then Elmer made string necklaces for horns and whistles for all the dragons and carefully tied them on. He wanted to take a really good look at the tremendous family, but they were near the entrance to the cave and he had to keep the flashlight in the knapsack. As he took out his cap pistol he asked, "Do you know how heavy the net is, and how it's fastened across the entrance?"

"No," answered the dragon father.

"Well, I'd better look," said Elmer. He quietly crept up toward the net, but the men were sitting close by and he didn't dare get near enough to see it well.

"We'll have to trust to luck," he told the dragons as he started back through the tunnel to Boris.

Chapter Ten

ESCAPE

"Boris! Boris!" whispered Elmer from under the snapdragon bush.

"Are they all right? What's happened?"

"Nothing's happened. Everyone's all right, and we're ready to go. I couldn't see the net, but we'll hope for the best. Did you say one of the men is called Frank?"

"Yes. I heard them mention a Frank and an Albert."

"Good. I'll meet you here afterwards. I told your family you'd have to take me back and that you'd find them near here someplace."

"Fine," said the dragon. "I can't wait."

"All right, now. I'm going back. Remember, as soon as you hear my cap pistol the third time, you're to make as much noise with the horn and whistle as you possibly can."

Elmer turned back down into the tunnel and hurried to the big cave. Everyone was ready. "Boris will be your signal," he explained. "As soon as you hear him blowing his horn and whistle, you're all to blow as hard as you can in every direction. I'll yell 'Boris' when it's time to charge, but look carefully at the net before you try to pass by. I don't know where the opening will be. Ready?" whispered Elmer, his heart pounding so hard he was sure it must echo through the cave.

"Ready!" whispered the fifteen waiting dragons.

Elmer crept up close to the net. The men were unrolling blankets and getting ready for the night. There was no moon.

"Perfect!" thought Elmer. He took out his cap pistol and fired it once. Then, "Help! Help!" he cried in a gruff voice. "Get me out of here. I'm trapped!"

The men jumped up, tripping all over their blankets and bumping into one another.

"What was that?"

"Somebody's in the cave!"

"Frank, Albert, help, help!" yelled Elmer again.

"Come on, let's hurry," said the men and they began moving great boulders off the edge of the net.

"So that's how they fastened down the bottom," thought Elmer. "That should make it easy." Then he shot off his pistol again, and cried, "They got me! Help!"

The men frantically rolled away the boulders. Just as they began pulling aside the heavy net, Elmer shot off the pistol for the third time and ran back into the cave.

Boris heard the third shot and began blowing his whistle and horn and running up and down over the meadow. As the noise echoed over the lake the fifteen trapped dragons started in on their whistles and horns.

Noise roared wildly through the cave, back and forth across the lake, and echoed madly around the circle of mountains.

Some of the men had started off when they heard Boris; the others who had been about to rescue Elmer ran out of the cave in terror.

Elmer shouted "Boris!" and raced back through the tunnel.

The fifteen dragons surged toward the entrance, found where the men had pulled aside the net and poured through the opening, trampling out the campfire as they came. Into the sky they zoomed, still blowing their whistles and horns. Then they disappeared

into the darkness, leaving thirteen men scattered over the meadows where they had fled, and three men sitting in the lake water where they had jumped.

"What happened?" said Frank to Albert.

Chapter Eleven

"THE DRAGON AFFAIR"

Elmer ran up to the tunnel to Boris and away they flew long before the noise had stopped echoing among the mountains.

"Well, that's that!" said Elmer, panting for breath and reaching for his second box of Fig Newtons.

"Gosh, Elmer, I can't thank you enough!" said the dragon.

"Never mind that. I never had so much fun in my life. But you'll have to hurry me back to Seaweed City. I've got to take the train home as fast as possible."

Over the desert they flew, and the wind grew stronger and stung Elmer's face.

"I think a storm's coming up," said the dragon. "I

can smell the sand in the air."

"Wonderful!" cried Elmer. "The men will have to leave Blueland, and maybe you'll never be bothered again."

Over Spiky Mountain Range they sped, reaching the outskirts of Seaweed City at midnight.

"How about leaving you on top of the monument?" suggested the dragon. "Then I won't have to land on the ground."

"Fine," said Elmer, and the dragon glided onto the top of Seaweed City Monument overlooking the center of the city.

"Goodbye for the last time," said Elmer. "I'm sorry that I never really got to see your family. They must be magnificent! But tell them from me that nobody will ever know more about them than they do right now, except for our friend the old alley cat. I'll tell her all about it."

"Goodbye! I'd better hurry home, too," sobbed the

happy baby dragon. He clumsily hugged Elmer, and off he flew.

Elmer finished up the Fig Newtons, saving one box for the train, and climbed down the monument. Quickly he walked to the railroad station and asked for a ticket to Nevergreen City.

"Isn't it rather late for a boy of your size to be taking the train alone?" asked the ticket agent.

"I suppose so," answered Elmer, giving the man $7.27.

The man shrugged his shoulders and handed Elmer a ticket. "I can't get used to boys these days," he muttered. "By the way, there's a train in twenty minutes. Gets you down in Nevergreen at noon."

"Thanks," said Elmer, jingling the nine cents he had left in his pocket as if he were used to taking trains in the middle of the night.

When the train thundered into the station Elmer climbed aboard. "What are you doing, running away from home?" asked the conductor suspiciously.

"Oh, no sir. On the contrary, I'm on my way there now," said Elmer, looking the conductor straight in the eye.

"Have it your own way," said the conductor, punching the ticket.

Elmer slept right through to Nevergreen City. He walked up the front steps of his home just as his mother was making herself some lunch. "Elmer, Elmer, you're back! But you look half-starved!"

"I am!" said Elmer, hugging his mother and sitting down at the table. He ate three bowls of tomato soup, five slices of pumpernickel bread, four glasses of milk, six fried eggs, and two huge pieces of sponge cake. Then he went to talk to the cat.

It wasn't until the next morning that the "dragon affair" came out in the "Nevergreen City News."

"Listen to this!" yelled Mr. Elevator, reading aloud at breakfast: " 'A fantastic and unexplainable escape took place in the great, high mountains of Blueland late Sunday night. Fifteen dragons, a wonder in themselves as they have long been believed extinct...' " and the newspaper story went on to tell about the brave men who had fought their way back through treacherous sandstorms to tell "the most momentous story of our time."

" 'Unbelievers who doubt this story,' " continued Mr.

Elevator, reading aloud from the paper, " 'will find it difficult to dismiss the following supporting evidence of the presence of dragons in this region.' " Then he proceeded to read about a ship stationed off the coast of Popsicornia which twice had sighted a strange flying beast, once with a boy atop it. And about a certain Mr. Wagonwheel who claimed also to have seen it twice, once on the ground near his farm, and once in the air with a boy aboard, over Seaweed City. And about Chester DeWitt, a small boy who also claimed he'd seen the dragon over the city the preceding Thursday evening. Lastly, there was a short bit about the conductor and the ticket agent, who wondered if the boy they had seen late Sunday night could have had anything to do with the case, and so on.

Mr. Elevator dropped the paper and stared at Elmer. "Did you have anything to do with all this? I just don't understand your strange trips away from home."

"Me?" said Elmer, choking on a piece of toast. "Why, Father, you don't mean you really believe all that nonsense, do you?"

THE END

About the Author and the Illustrator

RUTH STILES GANNETT wrote *My Father's Dragon* just a few years after her graduation from Vassar College in 1944. It was an immediate success, becoming a Newbery Honor Book, and was soon followed by two sequels, *Elmer and the Dragon* and *The Dragons of Blueland*. All three dragon stories have been continuously in print in the more than 35 years since their publication. The author's other books include *Katie and the Sad Noise* and *The Wonderful House-Boat-Train*. She is married to the artist and art historian Peter Kahn. They live in an old farmhouse near Ithaca, New York, and have seven daughters.

RUTH CHRISMAN GANNETT was already a well-established illustrator when she began collaborating with her stepdaughter on *My Father's Dragon* and its sequels. Her pictures for these books are perhaps her most enduring work. Her illustrations may also be seen in the first edition of John Steinbeck's *Tortilla Flat* and in *Miss Hickory* by Carolyn S. Bailey. Mrs. Gannett was married to the late Lewis Gannett, daily book critic for the *New York Herald Tribune*. She died in 1979.